Five reason

love Isadora

Meet the magical,
fang-tastic Isadora Moon!

Isadora's cuddly toy, Pink Rabbit,
has been magicked to life!

This is Isadora's
first ever sleepover—
she's so excited!

Isadora's family is crazy!

Enchanting
pink and black
pictures

What is your favourite thing to do at a sleepover?

In the middle of the night, grabbing all the pillows and having an epic pillow fight!
– Tilli

Telling each other scary stories!
– Matilda

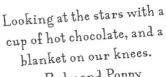

Looking at the stars with a cup of hot chocolate, and a blanket on our knees.
– Ruby and Poppy

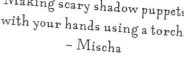

Making scary shadow puppets with your hands using a torch.
– Mischa

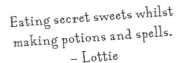

Eating secret sweets whilst making potions and spells.
– Lottie

Playing games and eating pink marshmallows.
– Roseanna

Family Tree

My Mum
Countess Cordelia
Moon

Baby Honeyblossom

My Dad
Count Bartholomew
Moon

Me!
Isadora Moon

Pink Rabbit

For vampires, fairies and humans everywhere!

And for my wonderful parents.

OXFORD
UNIVERSITY PRESS

Great Clarendon Street, Oxford OX2 6DP

Oxford University Press is a department of the University of Oxford.
It furthers the University's objective of excellence in research, scholarship, and
education by publishing worldwide. Oxford is a registered trade mark of Oxford
University Press in the UK and in certain other countries

First published 2019

British Library Cataloguing in Publication Data

Data available

ISBN: 978-0-19-276711-0

3 5 7 9 10 8 6 4 2

Printed in UK by Bell & Bain Ltd, Glasgow

Paper used in the production of this book is a natural,
recyclable product made from wood grown in sustainable forests.
The manufacturing process conforms to the environmental
regulations of the country of origin.

MIX
Paper from
responsible sources
FSC® C007785

ISADORA · MOON

Has a Sleepover

Harriet Muncaster

OXFORD
UNIVERSITY PRESS

Chapter ONE

'We're going to have a competition!'
Miss Cherry announced to the class, one
bright and flowery spring morning.
'A baking competition! It's going to be
like that programme you all watch on the
television, *Sponge and Sprinkles.*'

'Ooh,' said Oliver. 'I love that show!'
'Me too,' shouted Sashi excitedly.

'I watch it every week.'

'The winners,' continued Miss Cherry, 'will win tickets to the final of the show. You'll get to be in the audience and watch it in real life!'

'Eeee!' squealed Zoe, next to me. The class all started to chatter excitedly—

everyone except me. I didn't know anything about *Sponge and Sprinkles*. I don't even have a TV at home.

My mum is a fairy, you see—she loves being out in nature, and can't understand why humans like to 'sit in front of boxes with moving pictures on them'.

And even if we did have a TV, I would only be able to watch *Sponge and Sprinkles* while Dad was out of the house. For him, it would be a horror show. He is a vampire, and finds all food disgusting unless it is red.

'You will need to partner up,' said Miss Cherry. 'And try to bake the most spectacular cake you can! The best bake will win the tickets. You have all weekend to make your cakes, and I will judge them on Monday morning.'

'Eeee,' squealed Zoe again. 'This is so exciting! Isadora, you'll be my partner, won't you?'

'Of course,' I said, delighted. Zoe is

my best friend, apart from Pink Rabbit. He used to be my favourite stuffed toy, but my mum magicked him alive with her wand.

'I've got a good idea,' said Zoe. 'Why don't you come to my house on Saturday? We can bake the cake and then have a sleepover. It will be so fun. We can sleep in the same room and tell ghost stories and have a secret midnight feast!'

'I would love that,' I said. 'I've never been to a sleepover before.'

'I'll get my mum to ask your mum, after school, then,' said Zoe. 'Oh it will be SO fun. I can't wait!'

'We're going to have a sleepover, too,' said Oliver, from behind us. 'Bruno and I are going to make the best cake in the world.'

'It's going to be a dinosaur one,' said Bruno. 'With green—'

'Shh!' said Oliver. 'Don't tell them our plan.'

'Oops, sorry,' said Bruno, turning red. 'It's not going to be a dinosaur one.'

'It's OK,' said Zoe. 'Don't worry—we won't steal your idea. We have a much better one!'

'Do we?' I asked, as we packed up our things to go home.

'Well,' whispered Zoe, 'not yet. But we WILL!'

'Isadora's going on a sleepover,' said Mum at breakfast, that evening. We have two breakfasts in our house, because Dad sleeps through the day and wakes up at night.

'A sleepover?' asked Dad. 'Why?'

'For fun,' said Mum. 'Humans like them, apparently.'

'They do,' I said. 'My friends are always having sleepovers. Zoe says you get to stay up all night and have a midnight feast!'

'Oh?' asked Dad, confused. 'That just sounds like my normal life.' He continued to suck his red juice through a straw, making a horrible slurping sound. When he finished, he wiped his mouth and said: 'Humans are funny creatures.'

The next day, I spent the afternoon packing my bag for the sleepover. I wanted to make sure that I didn't forget anything. I put in my bat-patterned pyjamas, my slippers, my pillow, and my sleeping bag, from when we went camping.

'That should be everything,' I said to Pink Rabbit. 'Can you think of anything else?'

Pink Rabbit
pointed at my wand,
which was lying on my
bedside table. I picked it up and
added it to the things in my bag.

'Good thinking!' I said. 'It will be
useful to use as a torch.'

By the time I had finished packing my
bag, I was feeling a little bit nervous.

'Don't worry,' said Mum. 'I'm sure
you'll have a lovely time.'

'I'm sure I will,' I said in a small
voice. As we walked up the drive to Zoe's
front door, I suddenly wasn't sure if I

wanted to go at all.

'Maybe I shouldn't stay the night,' I said. 'Maybe I should just go for a few hours, and then you can pick me up?'

'If you like,' said Mum. 'But I think once you see Zoe, you'll change your mind. How about if I tell Dad to come and check on you tonight, during his nightly fly? He can wait in Zoe's garden, and if you're still awake at midnight you can look out of the window and wave to him to show you're OK.'

'Well, all right,' I said, feeling a lot better. Mum knocked on the door and we heard an excited pattering of footsteps coming towards it.

'Isadora!' shouted Zoe, when it
opened. She jumped on top of me and
gave me such a huge, squeezy hug that I
dropped my bag on the floor.

'Hello Isadora,' said Zoe's mum, smiling. She looked so friendly and welcoming that suddenly I didn't feel nervous any more. Mum kissed me goodbye, and I waved her off excitedly.

'Do you want to have some tea?' asked Zoe. 'I've got my special dolls' tea set out. It's all ready!' She led me through to the kitchen, where she had laid the table.

'Mum's let me make fairy bread, as a treat.'

'Fairy bread?' I asked, wondering what it was. I had never heard of it, even though my mum is a fairy.

'Yes,' said Zoe, sitting down on one of

the chairs. 'It's delicious, look!'

On the two small plates were slices of bread, buttered, and sprinkled all over with hundreds and thousands.

'I thought it would make you feel at home,' said Zoe, biting into hers, so that I could hear the hundreds and thousands crunching between her teeth. 'With you being half fairy and everything!'

'Thanks, Zoe,' I said, biting into my own piece of fairy bread. I didn't like to tell Zoe that this wasn't a real fairy thing. It must be something that humans had invented.

'It's yummy, isn't it?' said Zoe, crunching away.

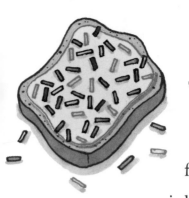

I nodded politely. My mouth was too full of butter and cake sprinkles to speak. The fairy bread was nice, but not quite as nice as my usual peanut-butter sandwich snack.

While we ate it, we watched the small television on the kitchen wall. An episode of *Sponge and Sprinkles* was on. Five people stood behind pale-pink counters, with mixing bowls and wooden spoons in their hands.

'Three, two, one, BAKE!' shouted the presenter, Whippy McFluff. She was so excited that her ice-cream swirl of hair was wobbling all over the place.

The contestants started furiously pouring
ingredients into their bowls. Butter, sugar,
flour, chocolate chips . . . Both of us sat
entranced, our eyes glued to the screen.

'Maybe we can get some inspiration
for our cake,' I said.

Whippy McFluff started to dance around the room, dipping her fingers into the contestants' bowls, and tasting their different mixtures.

'Lovely!' she cried. 'Ooh, zesty! Mmm . . . lemons.' She sent a beaming smile to the camera, all her white teeth flashing.

'She's so fun,' said Zoe. 'I would love to meet her.'

'Well, maybe we can,' I said. 'If we win the competition.'

Chapter TWO

When we had finished our tea, we went to find Zoe's mum.

'Can you help us with our cake now?' asked Zoe. 'We want to make one like the one we just saw on *Sponge and Sprinkles*!'

'It was huge,' I said. 'With five different layers—all different flavours. Coffee, chocolate, raspberry, lemon, and pumpkin!' I had never seen such a wonderful cake before.

Zoe's mum laughed. 'You'll need a lot of ingredients for a cake like that,' she said. 'I'll have to go to the supermarket, if you're serious.'

'We ARE serious,' said Zoe. 'We really want to win the tickets.'

Zoe's mum looked at her watch. 'Well, alright,' she said. 'I'll pop there now. We need some fish for dinner, anyway. Dad's in the garden, if you need anything.'

'Oh thank you,' said Zoe, jumping up and down.

While we waited for Zoe's mum to come back, we went up to Zoe's bedroom.

I love Zoe's bedroom, as it is always so interesting. She has butterflies painted on her walls and loads of posters stuck up on her wardrobe door. She also has the biggest dressing-up box of everyone I know.

'Shall we play dress-up?' I said, opening up the box and beginning to rummage inside.

'Sure!' said Zoe, taking out some pink fairy wings and a sparkly silver crown. She put them on, then added a pair of slip-on shoes with pom-poms on the toes.

'I know,' she said. 'Why don't I be a fairy queen, and you be a vampire queen? We can be best friends, but the rulers of different kingdoms. My kingdom will be on a fluffy, pink cloud! I'm going to have a palace there made from glass, and everything will smell of roses.' She began to spray herself all over with a flower-scented perfume.

'OK.' I said, taking a tall, shimmery, black crown out from the box and putting it on my head. 'My kingdom will be up in the night sky, surrounded by glittering stars, and I will have one hundred pet bats. And Pink Rabbit will be a vampire prince!'

Pink Rabbit looked pleased at my

suggestion, and began to hop up and down happily.

'Coco will be a fairy princess!' said Zoe, picking up her favourite toy monkey from her pillow and hugging it to her chest. Pink Rabbit watched interestedly. Then he bounced over to Zoe, and held out his paw.

'Pink Rabbit wants to shake Coco's hand,' I said.

Zoe knelt down, and held her monkey out to Pink Rabbit.

'Coco is pleased to meet you,' she said, and Pink Rabbit's ears twitched with happiness. He began to stroke Coco's stripy tail.

'I think they like each other,' I said.

'I think so, too!' laughed Zoe. Then a wistful look came over her face.

'Isadora,' she said. 'Do you think that maybe . . . maybe you could magic Coco alive, just for our game? I think Pink Rabbit would love it. And I would too!'

I glanced over at my wand, poking out from my bag in the corner of the room.

'I guess I could,' I replied, hurrying over to fetch it.

Zoe started to jump up and down with excitement.

'Could you?' she whispered breathlessly. 'Really?'

'I'll try,' I said. 'I've only done this spell once before, though. It might take me a few tries.' I pointed my wand at Coco the monkey, and squeezed my eyes tightly shut. I waved my wand, then opened my

eyes again. A stream of twinkly
sparks floated down onto Coco,
landing all over her fur.

'Ooh!' sighed Zoe, in wonder.

The sparks began to fade, and
underneath them, Coco blinked her
button eyes. The spell had worked
first time!

'Oh my,' squealed Zoe, her hand flying to her mouth in astonishment. Coco twitched her arms and then her tail. Then she stood up shakily on her furry legs, and jumped into Zoe's arms. Zoe hugged Coco tightly, and I could see tears shining in the corners of her eyes.

'Thank you,' she whispered. 'Thank you! Thank you!'

'That's OK,' I said, feeling pleased that Zoe was so happy. Pink Rabbit was happy, too. He was bouncing up and down by Zoe's feet, trying to get Coco's attention.

We began to play our game, pretending that Zoe's bed, with its pink duvet, was a fluffy, pink cloud. We laid out a black, starry cape from the dressing-up box, too. When I stood on top of it, I was in my vampire kingdom, inside my dark, gothic castle with my one hundred pet bats flapping around me.

'I'm going to fly to your palace now,' I said, and flapped into the air, flying the short distance across the floor and landing on Zoe's bed.

'I'm going to fly too,' said Zoe, flapping her pretend fairy wings and jumping down onto the floor. She stretched both her arms out wide and ran round the room in circles. Coco skipped along behind her, and Pink Rabbit followed.

'I'm flying through the sky,' she shouted. 'It's full of fluffy, pink clouds!' As I watched her, I had an idea. What a lovely surprise it would be for Zoe, if I magicked her pretend fairy wings to life!

When I was sure she wasn't looking, I waved my wand again. Sparks and glitter

flew through the air, and suddenly her
wings started to flap all on their own. Zoe
began to rise up towards the ceiling.

'Oh my goodness,' she squealed.
'Look at me!'

'You're *really* flying!' I laughed,
flapping my own wings and joining her in
the air.

41

Round and round the room we flew, until we got tired and landed back down on the bed with a bounce. As we did so, we heard the sound of a door opening downstairs.

'My mum must be back,' said Zoe. She grabbed my hand and we raced down the stairs together and into the kitchen, leaving Coco and Pink Rabbit playing in the bedroom.

'Gosh,' said Zoe's mum. 'You two look a little different from when I left!'

'I'm a fairy queen and Isadora's a vampire queen,' said Zoe.

'Well, if you two queens would care to wash your hands and put on some

aprons,' said Zoe's mum, 'we can start
making the cake!'

I felt a fizz of excitement, as Zoe's
mum started to lay out all the ingredients
on the table: flour, butter, sugar, and eggs.
There were little bottles of food colouring,
too, a slab of chocolate to be melted, and a
piping bag for the icing.

'It's like we're on *Sponge and Sprinkles*!' said Zoe, as she watched her mum measure out some sugar and butter and put them into two bowls. She gave one to Zoe and one to me, and we began to mix them with wooden spoons. It was harder than I thought it would be, because the butter was still very solid from being in the supermarket fridge.

'We could use your wand to help it along a bit,' whispered Zoe, when her mum's back was turned.

'Oh I don't know,' I said, jamming my spoon into a lump of hard butter. 'I'm not sure we should use my wand to make the cake. It might be cheating.'

'Not really,' said Zoe. 'It's only to make the butter softer. It will be just like using a food mixer! Our one is broken at the moment.'

'I suppose . . .' I said. 'OK, I'll go and fetch it.' I hurried out of the room and went back up to Zoe's bedroom.

Pink Rabbit and Coco were both sitting on the floor, looking at one of Zoe's books together. I grabbed my wand and ran back downstairs. As soon as Zoe's mum turned her back, I waved it over our mixing bowls. Sparks fizzed and twinkled, and suddenly the butter and sugar in our bowls became perfectly smooth and mixed.

'YES!' said Zoe. 'Perfect.'

'Wow,' said Zoe's mum, when she turned back round. 'Good job!'

She measured out some flour and poured it into our bowls. We mixed it in, together with some eggs.

'Now for the complicated part,' said Zoe's mum. 'If you want a five-layer cake,

we need to split the mixture into five
different bowls and then put a different
flavour in each of them.' She began to
separate out the mixture, while Zoe and I
watched. Then we helped her to squeeze
and zest a lemon for the first layer of the
cake.

'This is going to be so delicious!' I said.

After the lemon, we added some raspberries to the second bowl of mixture, and then chocolate chips and cocoa powder to the third. I chose pumpkin for the fourth layer and Zoe chose coffee for the fifth, even though she hates the smell.

'It's for Miss Cherry,' she explained. 'I know she loves coffee, because she always has a mug of it on her desk!'

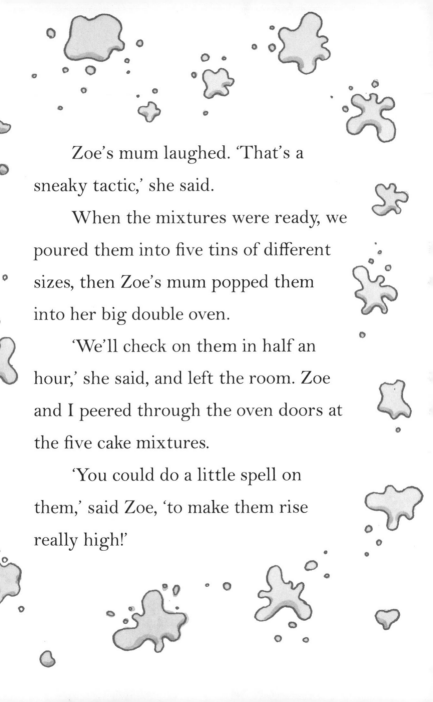

Zoe's mum laughed. 'That's a sneaky tactic,' she said.

When the mixtures were ready, we poured them into five tins of different sizes, then Zoe's mum popped them into her big double oven.

'We'll check on them in half an hour,' she said, and left the room. Zoe and I peered through the oven doors at the five cake mixtures.

'You could do a little spell on them,' said Zoe, 'to make them rise really high!'

'Ooh,' I said, a vision floating into my mind, of a cake almost taller than us. I waved my wand, and we watched as the cake mixture in the oven began to puff upwards, to twice the normal size.

'Wow,' said Zoe's mum when she came in to check on the cakes. 'Look how tall they are. Incredible!' She took them out of the oven and turned them out onto wire racks. They smelled delicious. While we waited for them to cool, Zoe's mum helped us to make the icing—a different colour for every layer! Then she left us to ice the cakes.

'This cake is going to look amazing!' said Zoe, as we began to spread the icing onto the cooled sponge. 'We're sure to win!'

'I hope so,' I said, opening a little pot of sprinkles, and shaking out tiny hearts and flowers onto the cake. Now that all the layers were on top of each other, it was so tall that Zoe and I couldn't see over the top.

'What would make it look really spectacular,' said Zoe, 'is if the icing was glittery. I've never seen glittery icing before.'

'Nor have I,' I said, 'but it's a great idea!' I waved my wand, so that the icing began to glitter. For good measure, I waved my wand over the sprinkles, too.

They began to sparkle, crackle, and pop, like tiny fireworks.

'AMAZING!' cried Zoe.

We continued to decorate the cake, adding some icing here and a few more sprinkles there, and piping swirls and twirls all around the edges. I waved my wand again, casting a few more tiny little spells, to add a bit more magic and flavour to our creation. When we had finished, we stood back and admired our handiwork.

'WOW,' said Zoe, her eyes glittering in the reflection of our magical cake. 'There's no way we won't win the competition!'

She began to happily dance around the room.

'We're going to win the tickets,' she sang. 'We're going to meet Whippy McFluff!'

I laughed, feeling really happy that Zoe was so pleased.

'Oh my goodness,' gasped Zoe's mum, when she came into the kitchen a while later. 'What a sensational cake!' She walked around it, marvelling at all the little details.

'I didn't realize I bought glittery icing,' she said.

'It didn't say so on the packet. And look at those sprinkles – they're spinning around like miniature pinwheel fireworks. How clever!'

Zoe beamed, but I started to feel uncomfortable. Maybe we had got a little carried away with the wand waving.

Chapter THREE

After dinner, Zoe and I ran upstairs to her bedroom. It was dark outside now, and time to get ready for bed.

'Let's lay out all your night things,' said Zoe excitedly. We opened my bag together and unrolled my sleeping bag.

'Do you have a mattress?' asked Zoe. 'Or shall I ask my mum for one?'

'I've got one,' I said. I rummaged in my bag, and took out a little velvet pouch.

'That's tiny!' said Zoe. 'How can you fit a whole mattress in there?'

'It's a fairy one,' I said, opening the pouch and pulling out a small, fluffy, pink cloud. As soon as it was out in the air, the cloud began to grow bigger and bigger, until it was as big as a double bed and all squashy. Pink Rabbit and Coco immediately leaped up onto it, and began to jump up and down.

'Ooh,' said Zoe. 'It looks so comfy!'

'You can share it with me, if you like,' I said. 'There's plenty of room!' Zoe pulled her duvet from her bed and laid it next to

my sleeping bag, on top of the cloud.

'Oh this is so exciting,' she said. 'I love sleepovers!' We both bounced up and down on the cloud for a bit with Pink Rabbit and Coco, as it was so squashy, and then we went into the bathroom to get ready for bed.

'Oh no,' I said, suddenly remembering something. 'I forgot my toothbrush!'

'Don't worry,' said Zoe, opening a drawer underneath the sink. 'We have a spare head.'

'A spare head?' I asked. 'What do you mean?'

Zoe handed me a big chunky toothbrush with a button on it.

'It's electric,' she said. 'I've put the spare head on it. Press the button!'

I pressed the button and the toothbrush immediately began to vibrate furiously in my hand.

'Oh!' I said in surprise. I had never seen an electric toothbrush before. Dad

would be very interested in this. I tried to
squeeze some toothpaste onto the brush,
but it was vibrating so fast that bits just
kept whizzing right off it and splatting
onto the walls.

'Hang on,' said Zoe, taking the
toothbrush from me and turning it off.

'You have to put it in your mouth first, before you turn it on.'

She squeezed some toothpaste onto the brush and I put it into my mouth and pressed the button. My whole head began to vibrate and my vision started to shake, but when I had finished my fangs had never felt so clean!

'I'll have to tell my dad about these,' I said. 'He's always interested in new grooming products.'

'Do you want to do a face mask?' asked Zoe, opening the drawer again and getting out two small packets. 'I've seen my mum do them. I'm sure she won't mind.' She opened one of the little packets and took out a wet sheet of paper with two holes in it. It smelled of cucumbers. She put the sheet over her face so that only her eyes were poking out of the holes.

'You look like a ghost!' I squealed, opening my own packet and putting the mask onto my face. It was cool and made my cheeks tingle. We both peered into the mirror.

'I don't know why grown ups do these silly things,' said Zoe. 'We look so freaky!'

'Maybe it's because they secretly like dressing up, too,' I said. 'We look like ghosts!' We began to dance around and put our hands up in the air like claws.

'Oooooh!' wailed Zoe. 'I'm coming to get you!' She chased me out of the bathroom and back across the landing to her bedroom.

'What's going on up there?' called Zoe's mum, from down below. 'It's time to get into bed, girls!'

Zoe whipped the mask off her face and scrunched it up. I did the same and

by the time Zoe's mum came up to say
goodnight we were both lying quietly in
bed, side by side, with Pink Rabbit and
Coco snuggled between us.

'Goodnight, girls,' she said, turning off the light and closing the door. 'Sleep well!'

'Night, Mum,' said Zoe.

We lay there in the dark for a bit, although it wasn't properly dark because Zoe had a night light plugged into the wall.

'We need to stay awake,' she whispered, 'so that we can get up for a midnight feast!'

'Ooh yes,' I said. 'What shall we have?'

'Cake,' suggested Zoe, giggling.

'We can't eat the cake!'

'I know—I was only joking. We'll

have to find something else. Maybe we can eat the rest of the sprinkles . . .'

'Maybe,' I said, my mind drifting back to the cake. I was starting to feel a little bit bad. I kept thinking of Oliver and Bruno, and how excited they had been about their dinosaur cake. I knew they would have put a lot of hard work into it.

'Zoe,' I whispered.

'What?'

'I don't think we should enter our cake in the competition.'

'Why not?' said Zoe, sitting bolt upright in the bed. 'Of course we should enter our cake!'

'But we cheated,' I said. 'We used

magic. I've been thinking about it all evening. I don't think it would be fair!'

'It was only a little bit of magic,' said Zoe, in a quiet voice.

'It was more than a little bit,' I said. 'And, really, we shouldn't have used any at all. We were having so much fun that we got carried away.'

'But we HAVE to enter the cake,' said Zoe again. 'We want to meet Whippy McFluff, don't we?'

'Well, yes . . .' I said. 'I just—'

'Oh I *really* want to win and meet Whippy McFluff,' said Zoe, starting to sound a bit upset.

'OK,' I sighed, not wanting to ruin

the sleepover with an argument. I tried to change the subject instead.

'How are we going to keep ourselves awake?' I asked. 'For the midnight feast?'

'By telling ghost stories!' said Zoe, perking up again and giving a little shiver. She lit a torch and put it under her chin.

'I'll start,' she said, and she began to tell a story. It was about an old woman who trailed the streets of our town after dark, dragging chains behind her that clinked and clanked all night long.

'That sounds a bit unrealistic,' I said, thinking about the friendly ghost, Oscar, who lived in my attic at home. 'Let me tell you about my real ghost!'

'But Oscar's not scary,' said Zoe. 'Ghost stories have to be scary. That's the point of them.'

'Oh,' I said, confused.

'Never mind,' said Zoe. 'Let's talk about our biggest wishes instead. Do you know what mine is?'

'To meet Whippy McFluff?'

'Close, but no,' said Zoe. 'My biggest wish is that we can stay best friends for ever! And when we grow up, we can live in houses next door to each other.'

'Oh Zoe,' I said. 'That's a lovely wish! I hope it comes true.'

Zoe smiled and hugged Coco, who was snuggled up in her arms.

'What's yours?' she asked. 'We need to keep talking, so that we can stay awake until midnight.'

'Hmm,' I said, 'let me just think about it.' The room went quiet for a moment, and all I could hear was the tick-tock of the clock.

'I know,' I said at last. 'Apart from staying *your* best friend for ever, my biggest wish is to become a famous ballerina. A vampire fairy ballerina!'

But Zoe didn't reply. She had closed her eyes and gone to sleep, tightly hugging Coco the monkey—who had fallen asleep, too.

'I suppose we won't be having the midnight feast after all,' I whispered to Pink Rabbit, and I closed my eyes as well.

But it was difficult to fall asleep. The little creaks and noises of the night sounded different in Zoe's house, and I wasn't used to having a night light in my bedroom. Also, I was still feeling worried about the cake, and about how we had cheated by using my magic wand. The more I thought about it, the guiltier I felt.

I was still awake, worrying, when Zoe's glow-in-the-dark clock showed that it was midnight. Quietly, I slipped out of bed and pattered over to the window. I peered out into the dark garden, but couldn't see Dad. Maybe he had forgotten.

Then I looked upwards into the sky
and saw a black shape soaring towards the
house, in the light of the fingernail moon. I
opened the window as softly as possible, and
climbed out, flapping my wings and flying
over to meet Dad in the middle of the air.

'Hey!' he said. 'I thought you would be
asleep by now.'

'I couldn't sleep,' I told him.

We flew up to the roof of the house
together, and sat on the sloped tiles. Dad
wrapped me in his cape, and we looked at the
stars for a while.

'So tell me why you can't sleep,' said
Dad. 'Is it because everything is different at
Zoe's house?'

'Well, it is different,' I said.
'They have night lights and electric
toothbrushes, and a television in the
kitchen. But that's not why I can't
sleep.'

'Oh?' said Dad.

'We made our cake for the
competition,' I explained, 'but we
used my magic wand to make it
look really incredible. And now . . .
if we win, it will only be because
we cheated. And it won't be fair on
the others. I don't know what to do,

because Zoe really wants to enter the cake, but I don't think we should.'

'I see your problem,' said Dad. 'Do you remember when your cousin Mirabelle persuaded you to take a dragon to school, and got you into all sorts of trouble?'

I nodded.

'Well, this is a similar situation,' said Dad. 'It's important to stand up for what you believe in. If you don't think it's right to take the cake into school, then you mustn't let Zoe push you

into it. Even if she is your best friend and you want to make her happy. I'm sure she knows, deep down, that it would be wrong.'

'Really?' I said, feeling loads better. 'Do you think so?'

'I'm sure of it,' said Dad. He smiled and ruffled my messy hair. 'Now tell me a bit more about these electric toothbrushes!'

Chapter FOUR

It was almost one o'clock in the morning
when I flew back into Zoe's room and
closed the window gently behind me. I
slipped back into the big, squashy cloud-
bed, and snuggled down with Pink Rabbit.
This time, I had no trouble getting to
sleep. I closed my eyes, and the next time I
opened them it was morning and sunlight

was streaming through the window.

'Wakey wakey!' said Zoe, who was already up and bouncing about her room with Coco the monkey. She was busy getting out all her dolls' clothes and laying them out on the floor.

'Which outfit do you want to wear, Coco?' she asked. 'The stripy dress or the Babygro?'

Coco leaped across the room and up onto the wardrobe. She did not want to wear any clothes!

It seemed to be a long time before Zoe's mum called us down for breakfast, and by the time we walked into the kitchen, my tummy was rumbling.

'My parents like to have a lie in at the weekend,' explained Zoe.

Breakfast at Zoe's was very different to how we have it in my house. We usually have toast and fairy-flower nectar yoghurt, and red juice for Dad, but in Zoe's house it was bacon, eggs, mushrooms, tomatoes, sausages, and orange juice.

'Yum!' I said. As we ate, I stared at

the cake sitting on the counter behind the table. When we had finished our breakfast and cleared away, I grabbed Zoe's arm.

'We really can't enter the cake,' I said. 'It wouldn't be fair.'

'But—' began Zoe, looking disappointed.

'It would be cheating,' I said. 'It would be awful if we won. Think about it.'

'I suppose . . .' said Zoe. She looked down at her hands and twisted them about. 'We won't enter it,' she said. 'But can we make another one before you go home? Without magic.'

'Gosh!' said Zoe's mum, when we asked her to help us. 'Another cake? You must have really enjoyed making the first one.'

'We did,' I said, because it was completely true.

For the next few hours, we stayed in the kitchen and used up the rest of the

ingredients from the day before, making
another cake. It was much smaller and not
nearly as impressive as the first one, but
I felt much happier about entering it into
the competition.

'I'll bring it in on Monday,' said Zoe, as I packed up my things to go home. She helped me squish the magic fairy-cloud back into its tiny pouch.

'I've had the best time,' she said. 'It's been the best sleepover ever!'

'It has!' I agreed, giving her a big hug. 'Thank you for having me.'

'Thank you for magicking my monkey,' said Zoe, stroking Coco, who was sitting on her shoulder. 'I know I only asked you to magic her alive for our game, but can she stay alive for always?'

'For always,' I promised.

'I'll have to explain that to my parents, somehow,' said Zoe, and we both

giggled. Then I picked up my suitcase, and
we went downstairs.

'Did you have a lovely time?' asked
Mum, as we walked home together.

'The loveliest time!' I said, and I told
her all about the two cakes we had made.

The next day at school, there was
an excited chatter in the classroom. My
friends had all brought in their cakes and
were lining them up on a big table at the
back of the classroom.

'Goodness me,' Miss Cherry was
saying. 'I'm going to have trouble
choosing the winner.'

I scurried over to have a look at

the cakes that had already been brought
in. Sashi and Samantha had made one in
the shape of a flower, with little butterflies
perched all over it. It was very pretty.
Dominic and Jasper had made a cake
shaped like a robot, covered in grey
icing, with jelly sweets for buttons.
In the middle of the table stood Bruno
and Oliver's dinosaur cake. I could tell

they had put more effort into theirs than anyone else. They had made a sponge stegosaurus covered in green icing, with triangle biscuit spikes stuck all the way along its back.

They had modelled little trees and smaller dinosaurs out of icing, and placed them around the stegosaurus to make an edible landscape. When I saw it, I felt more relieved than ever that Zoe was bringing the new cake and not the one full of magic. I wondered where she was. It was not like her to be late for school.

'Sorry, Miss Cherry!' came a voice from the doorway, and Zoe came into the room, carrying a huge cake. It was a

towering, magical cake with glittery icing
and tiny pinwheel fireworks spinning and
sparkling all over it. A cake with five tall
layers, each one a different flavour.

I stared at her and at the cake. My mouth fell open in horror, and I grabbed on to Pink Rabbit's paw.

'Wow!' said Miss Cherry, her eyes almost popping out of her head with amazement. She hurried over to help Zoe lift the cake onto the table. It stood there like a mountain, looming above Bruno and Oliver's dinosaur cake.

'I'm sorry,' whispered Zoe, when she came to sit down next to me. 'I just couldn't resist it this morning. I saw the two cakes sitting side by side on the counter, and this one just looked so much better!'

'But—' I said, starting to feel cross and upset.

'Don't be cross,' Zoe begged. She reached out for my hand under the desk, but I snatched it away. I felt like she had betrayed me.

'Isadora . . .' Zoe whispered, her voice sounding a little wobbly now. 'I'm sorry. I just—'

'Quiet, please!' said Miss Cherry, holding her hands up for silence in the classroom. 'It's time to taste-test the cakes!' She went over to the table and cut a small slice out of each of them.

'Mmm,' she said as she nibbled and chewed. 'Lovely!' When she got to our cake, she took a tiny slice for each layer and tasted them all. Her eyes went big and round.

'My goodness!' she said. 'These flavours are sensational. The sprinkles are just POPPING in my mouth!'

'See?' whispered Zoe next to me, but she didn't sound so sure now.

'I declare Zoe and Isadora the winners!' said Miss Cherry, taking an envelope from her pocket and holding it up in the air. 'The tickets are yours!'

Zoe stood up and walked over to the table. I followed her, my cheeks burning with shame. She took the tickets and held them in her hands.

'Your cake is a work of art,' said Miss Cherry. 'It must have taken you all weekend.'

'It did,' said Zoe, but her voice sounded choked now. I looked across to where Bruno and Oliver were sitting. They were clapping along with the others, but I could see the disappointment in their faces.

'Well done, both of you!' said Miss Cherry, smiling. 'Now, I think we'll all have a slice of cake.' She began to cut the cakes up into little squares and put them on plates. As she did so, the class chattered.

'You can go and sit down now,' Miss Cherry said to us, and Zoe started to walk back towards our tables, clutching the tickets in her hand. I followed her, still feeling angry and upset. I wondered if I should go back and tell Miss Cherry that we had cheated.

But just as Zoe got back to her chair, she stopped and stood very still for a moment. Then she turned round

98

and walked back to the table where Miss Cherry was cutting the cakes. I followed.

'Miss Cherry?' she whispered. 'I need to tell you something.'

'Yes?'

'Isadora and I don't deserve to win the tickets.'

'What do you mean?' Miss Cherry stopped cutting a petal off Sashi and Samantha's flower cake, and looked up.

'We, um . . . cheated,' said Zoe, in a small voice. 'The cake wasn't all our own work. We used Isadora's wand to make some of it.'

'Oh,' said Miss Cherry. She sounded disappointed.

'I'm really sorry,' said Zoe. 'It was my fault. Isadora didn't want to enter the cake, but I brought it in anyway.'

'I see,' said Miss Cherry. 'What a shame.' She didn't seem cross, but she held her hand out for the tickets and Zoe gave them back.

'I will have to judge again,' she said.

'I know,' said Zoe, staring down at the floor. I saw a little tear escape from her eye.

'Now, now,' said Miss Cherry. 'We all do things we shouldn't, sometimes. And you did the right thing in owning up.'

Zoe sniffed.

'And, winners or not, we can all enjoy some delicious cake now.' She gave one of the plates to Zoe and one to me. We went back to our desks and sat down. I reached out, squeezed Zoe's hand, and gave her a big beaming smile.

'Right!' said Miss Cherry. 'There's been a change of plan. For reasons that I won't discuss, Zoe and Isadora have been disqualified from the competition. The new winners are . . . Bruno and Oliver!'

'YES!' shouted Bruno and Oliver, both leaping up from their chairs and dancing around the room. They looked so pleased and delighted that I felt a glow of happiness warm my whole body.

'WOOHOO!' shouted Oliver, waving the tickets in the air.

'It really is a most fabulous dinosaur cake,' said Miss Cherry. 'The best I've ever seen!'

Zoe looked down at her hands, and I knew she was feeling a bit sad about not winning the tickets and getting to meet Whippy McFluff.

'I'll tell you what,' I said. 'Why don't you come round to mine next weekend, for a sleepover? You can bring Coco and we can make real magic fairy cakes with my mum. Then I'll get my dad to take us out for a proper vampire midnight feast on the roof of our house, and we can go for a fly among the stars!'

Zoe looked up, her eyes sparkling.

'I would love that!' she said, throwing
her arms around my neck and giving me
a huge, squishy hug. 'There's nothing I'd
like to do more.'

Turn the page for
some fun things
to make and do,
inspired by
Isadora and Zoe's
sleepover!

Make a fangtastic three-layer cake!

This cake might not be *quite* as big as Isadora and Zoe's cake, but it will still be spectacular!

What you will need:

For cake:

★ 225g butter, softened

★ 225g caster sugar

★ 4 large free-range eggs, lightly beaten

★ 200g self-raising flour, sifted

★ 0.5 tsp baking powder

★ 2 tbsp cocoa powder

★ 1 tsp vanilla extract

★ 75g fresh raspberries

What you will need:

For icing:

- ⭐ 500g icing sugar
- ⭐ 250g unsalted butter
- ⭐ 1 tsp vanilla extract
- ⭐ 1 tbsp whole milk

Method:

1. Preheat the oven to 180°C, fan 160°C, gas 4.

2. Grease and line the base of three 20cm round cake tins.

3. Cream the butter and sugar together in a large bowl with an electric whisk until the mixture is pale and fluffy.

4. Slowly add the eggs, beating all the time, then fold in the flour and baking powder.

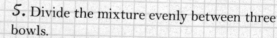

5. Divide the mixture evenly between three bowls.

6. Put the raspberries in a blender and whizz until smooth. Pass through a sieve to get rid of the pips. Add this puree to one of the bowls.

7. Mix the cocoa powder with 3 tablespoons of boiling water then add this into the mixture in the second bowl.

8. Add the vanilla extract to the third bowl.

9. Spoon the mixture from each bowl into a tin and bake for around 20 minutes until lightly golden and a skewer inserted into the middle comes out clean.

10. Remove from the oven and set aside for five minutes, then turn out onto a wire rack and let them cool completely. Don't forget to remove the paper!

Make sure the cakes are completely cool before you start decorating, otherwise the icing will melt and drip off!

11. With an electric whisk beat the butter for about five minutes, until it is light and creamy.

12. Slowly add the icing sugar one spoon at a time, continuing to beat.

13. Add in the milk and vanilla extract, still beating all the time. The longer you beat your buttercream for, the lighter and airier it will be.

14. Now you can start to build your cake! Spread the buttercream on two of your cakes and sandwich the three cakes together.

15. Starting at the top, cover the whole cake with a layer of icing, and chill in the fridge for 15 minutes. This will seal in the crumbs.

16. Cover the whole cake with another layer of icing.

17. Cover it with sprinkles, flowers, glitter, and anything else you can think of, or just leave it as it is.

18. Chill for another 30 minutes to set the icing.

19. ENJOY!

Build a story!

At the sleepover, Isadora and Zoe try to stay awake until midnight by telling ghost stories. Play this fun game, for two people or more, to make up your own stories! (They don't have to be scary if you don't want them to be.)

1. Sit in a circle (or facing each other if there are just two of you).

2. Choose someone to go first. That person starts the story 'Once upon a time . . .' and completes the sentence.

3. The next person must continue the story, adding just one sentence.

4. Keep going round, until the story
is complete!

This game is a great way to come up with some
hilarious stories, and you can play as many
times as you like. Write down your favourite
stories, so you don't forget them!

Which kind of cake are you?

Take the quiz to find out!

What is your favourite kind of cake?

A. I can't choose—they're all so tasty!

B. Madeira cake, it's good for carving into shapes.

C. Victoria sponge.

What do you think is the best cake size?

A. Gigantic! The bigger the better.

B. Middle-sized cakes are the best.

C. I prefer a small cake—it means I can eat it all!

What is the best cake topping?

A. Colourful sprinkles, swirly icing, glitter, and sparklers. And a bit more glitter.

B. My own models made out of icing and biscuits.

C. A simple dusting of icing sugar.

Results

Mostly As

You are Isadora and Zoe's sensational layer cake! You love to be centre of attention, and think there's nothing better than sparkles and glitter!

Mostly Bs

You are Bruno and Oliver's dinosaur cake! You love being creative and making things with your hands.

Mostly Cs

You are Isadora and Zoe's second cake! You don't like to be too flashy, and you think simplicity, honesty, and tastiness are the most important things in life.

Many more magical stories to collect!

Harriet Muncaster

Harriet Muncaster, that's me! I'm the
author and illustrator of Isadora Moon.
Yes really! I love anything teeny tiny,
anything starry, and everything glittery.

Love Isadora Moon?
Why not try these too...

HORACE & Harriet

Friends, Romans, statues!

WRITTEN AND ILLUSTRATED BY THE SPLENDIFEROUS CLARE ELSOM

Dr Kitty Cat
is ready to rescue

Bramble
the Hedgehog

Jane Clarke

Magical Kingdom of Birds
The Missing Fairy-Wrens

ANNE BOOTH
Illustrated by Rosie Butcher

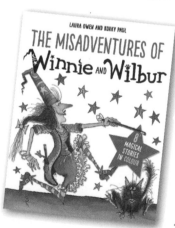

LAURA OWEN AND KORKY PAUL

THE MISADVENTURES OF
Winnie AND Wilbur

8 MAGICAL STORIES IN COLOUR

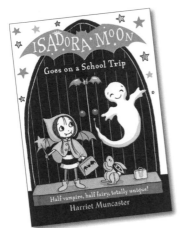
ISADORA MOON
Goes on a School Trip
Half vampire, half fairy, totally unique!
Harriet Muncaster

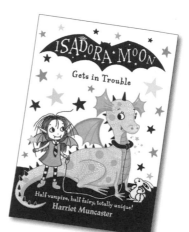
ISADORA MOON
Gets in Trouble
Half vampire, half fairy, totally unique!
Harriet Muncaster

ISADORA MOON
Goes to the Fair
Half vampire, half fairy, totally unique!
Harriet Muncaster

ISADORA MOON
Makes Winter Magic
Plus fangtastic activities!
Half vampire, half fairy, totally unique!
Harriet Muncaster